HUMPHREY CARPENTER

Mr Majeika and the School Trip

Illustrated by Frank Rodgers

PUFFIN

*With thanks to Eleanor Henderson, who asked
for another Mr Majeika book, and to St Ebbe's First
School, Oxford, who were the first audience for it –
and special thanks to the person who thought of
the rubber duck*

PUFFIN BOOKS

Published by the Penguin Group
Penguin Books Ltd, 80 Strand, London WC2R 0RL, England
Penguin Putnam Inc., 375 Hudson Street, New York, New York 10014, USA
Penguin Books Australia Ltd, 250 Camberwell Road, Camberwell,
Victoria 3124, Australia
Penguin Books Canada Ltd, 10 Alcorn Avenue, Toronto, Ontario, Canada M4V 3B2
Penguin Books India (P) Ltd, 11 Community Centre, Panchsheel Park,
New Delhi – 110 017, India
Penguin Books (NZ) Ltd, Cnr Rosedale and Airborne Roads, Albany, Auckland,
New Zealand
Penguin Books (South Africa) (Pty) Ltd, 24 Sturdee Avenue, Rosebank 2196, South Africa

Penguin Books Ltd, Registered Offices: 80 Strand, London WC2R 0RL, England

www.penguin.com

First published 1999
002

Text copyright © Humphrey Carpenter, 1999
Illustrations copyright © Frank Rodgers, 1999
All rights reserved

The moral right of the author and illustrator has been asserted

Printed in England by Clays Ltd, St Ives plc

British Library Cataloguing in Publication Data
A CIP catalogue record for this book is available from the British Library

ISBN-13: 978–0–141–34699–1

www.greenpenguin.co.uk

MIX
Paper from
responsible sources
FSC FSC® C018179
www.fsc.org

Penguin Books is committed to a sustainable
future for our business, our readers and our planet.
This book is made from Forest Stewardship
Council™ certified paper.

PUFFIN BOOKS

MR MAJEIKA AND THE SCHOOL TRIP

Humphrey Carpenter (1946–2005), the author and creator of *Mr Majeika*, was born and educated in Oxford. He went to a school called the Dragon School where exciting things often happened and there were some very odd teachers – you could even call it magical! He became a full-time writer in 1975 and was the author of many award-winning biographies. As well as the *Mr Majeika* titles, his children's books also included *Shakespeare Without the Boring Bits* and *More Shakespeare Without the Boring Bits*. He wrote plays for radio and theatre and founded the children's drama group The Mushy Pea Theatre Company. He played the tuba, double bass, bass saxophone and keyboard.

Humphrey once said, "The nice thing about being a writer is that you can make magic happen without learning tricks. Words are the only tricks you need. I can write: 'He floated up to the ceiling, and a baby rabbit came out of his pocket, grew wings, and flew away.' And you will believe that it really happened! That's magic, isn't it?"

Books by Humphrey Carpenter

MR MAJEIKA

MR MAJEIKA AND THE DINNER LADY

MR MAJEIKA AND THE GHOST TRAIN

MR MAJEIKA AND THE HAUNTED HOTEL

MR MAJEIKA AND THE MUSIC TEACHER

MR MAJEIKA AND THE SCHOOL BOOK WEEK

MR MAJEIKA AND THE SCHOOL CARETAKER

MR MAJEIKA AND THE SCHOOL INSPECTOR

MR MAJEIKA AND THE SCHOOL PLAY

MR MAJEIKA AND THE SCHOOL TRIP

MR MAJEIKA ON THE INTERNET

MR MAJEIKA VANISHES

MR MAJEIKA AND THE LOST SPELL BOOK

THE PUFFIN BOOK OF CLASSIC
CHILDREN'S STORIES (Ed.)

SHAKESPEARE WITHOUT THE BORING BITS

MORE SHAKESPEARE WITHOUT THE
BORING BITS

Contents

1. Who's For Lunch?

"I have an exciting announcement for Class Three," said Mr Potter, the head teacher of St Barty's School, at assembly one morning in April. "You'll all be going off for three days to an outdoor activity centre to do all sorts of exciting things."

"Hooray!" shouted almost everybody in Class Three, though they weren't quite sure what an outdoor activity centre was, or what kind of exciting things Mr Potter meant.

The only person who didn't cheer was

the worst-behaved boy in Class Three, Hamish Bigmore. "Boo!" he said loudly.

"Now, Hamish," said Mr Potter crossly, "don't be so silly. There's a big river at the outdoor activity centre, and you'll be able to go swimming and canoeing and caving."

"What's caving, Mr Potter?" asked Jody, who was standing next to Hamish.

"It's very exciting, Jody," said Mr Potter. "You go into a hole in the ground and you follow an underground passage until you get into a cave."

"That's not exciting," grumbled Hamish. "That's *boring*. Who wants to go poking about in a smelly old cave?"

But everyone else in Class Three was very pleased. So was their teacher, Mr Majeika.

"It'll be fun," he said. "I used to live in a

cave myself, when I was young and was still learning my spells."

Class Three liked hearing about what Mr Majeika had done before he came to St Barty's, because he hadn't been a teacher then. He'd been a wizard.

"Was it a nice cave, Mr Majeika?" asked Thomas and Pete, the twins.

"Very nice," said Mr Majeika. "The walls were covered in bright-green slime, and there was a family of bats living in the roof of the cave."

"Yuck!" said Jody. "It sounds horrid. I don't think I want to go into a cave if it's going to be like that."

"Class Four went to the outdoor activity centre last year," said Pete. "There was a very narrow passage into one of the caves, and their teacher, Mr Hodgkiss, got stuck. It was ages before they could get him out."

Hamish's eyes brightened. "Ah," he said. "I want to go caving after all. I can't wait till Mr Majeika gets stuck." Hamish was the only person in Class Three who didn't like Mr Majeika. This was because when Hamish was naughty Mr Majeika used spells to punish him.

"Mr Majeika won't get stuck," said Jody. "He's not as fat as Mr Hodgkiss. And if he does, he can use magic to get free."

"Huh," said Hamish. "We'll see."

It was a very warm day when the bus taking Class Three to the outdoor activity centre set out from St Barty's. In fact, it was soon uncomfortably hot.

"Phew," said Pete, taking off his anorak and pullover, and opening the Coke that he had brought in his packed lunch. "If I'd known it was going to be as hot as this, I'd have brought lots more to drink."

"Me too," said Jody, looking out of the window. "It's weeks since we had any rain. Look how brown and dried up the grass is."

For a while they looked at books and magazines, and the people who had brought Walkmans listened to music. After about an hour, the bus started to jerk a bit, and then it suddenly stopped.

"Oh dear," said the driver. "Something has gone wrong with the engine. And we're in the middle of nowhere."

They looked out of the bus windows and could see that he was right. There were no houses, just open countryside, with the fields so brown and dry that it looked like a sandy desert.

"I'll have to walk down the road to see if I can get help," said the driver. "But it's ages since we passed a house. It may take me some time."

Melanie, who always started to cry when anything went wrong, went "Boo-hoo!" and complained: "I'm thirsty. I want something to drink." Everyone else felt thirsty too.

"Mr Majeika," said Jody, "do you

remember when you were teaching us about the Sahara Desert, you told us that there was something called an oasis – a place in the middle of the desert with lots of water and nice things to eat? I wish we had one of those here, right now."

"An oasis?" said Mr Majeika. "Well, as it happens, I did once know a spell for making an oasis in the middle of a desert. It's quite a tricky one and I'm not sure that I remember it, but I'll have a go."

He muttered some strange words and suddenly everything went very bright. The sun had been hot before, but now it was like a raging furnace. Outside the windows of the bus, the brown fields turned even drier and became powdery yellow sand.

"Well, there's the desert," said Mr Majeika. "But I can't see the oasis."

"I can," called Thomas. "Look!"

Sure enough, a little distance away, there was a group of palm trees standing around a small lake of shining water. Everyone got out of the bus and ran over to it through the hot sand.

"Wow!" said Pete, as they drank from the cool waters of the lake. "And look, there's a sign saying 'Abdul's Motor Repairs – Cars and Buses Mended'."

"You're brilliant, Mr Majeika," said Jody. "That means we can get the bus mended too. What a wonderful start to our trip."

"Yes," said Thomas. "And I'm sure the outdoor activity centre will be just as exciting as this."

But it wasn't. When they got there they saw it was just a group of ordinary buildings, a bit like school. And the man in charge was very gloomy.

"Didn't you get my message?" he said.
"We phoned to say it hasn't rained for
weeks and the river has dried up."

Sure enough, outside the centre's
buildings, there was a broad river bed,
but only a trickle of water was running
down the middle of it.

"We won't be able to canoe on that, will
we?" asked Jody.

The man shook his head. "There's not even enough water for swimming," he said.

"Never mind," said Pete. "We'll just spend all the time caving. I can't wait to get into those caves. It'll be really exciting!"

"I'm afraid you can't," said the man. "There's been a fall of rock at the mouth of the caves and no one can get in. The only thing you'll be able to do is go for long walks."

"Oh dear," said Jody, and Hamish Bigmore shouted angrily: "I told you it would be boring. I want to go home."

"Hang on, Hamish," said Thomas. "Give Mr Majeika a chance. Look how he saved us all from being thirsty by making that oasis. I'm sure he can think of something else to stop our trip being dull. Can't you, Mr Majeika?"

"I'll do my best," said Mr Majeika. "But it won't be easy. In fact, it will probably take all night. The best thing you can all do is go to bed. I'll see what I can manage by the morning."

They slept very well, and Jody dreamed that Hamish Bigmore had turned into a hard-boiled egg, which everyone was trying to catch and put into a tin, but it kept bouncing around and shouting: "You can't eat me, my shell is too hard."

When she woke in the morning, she thought she must still be dreaming because there were strange noises all around her – a sort of scratchy, squeaking sound and also some low grunts and the slurping of water.

Opening her eyes fully, she looked out of the window and saw that everything outside the outdoor activity centre had changed. Yesterday there had been a road with cars passing by, with the dried-up river bed beyond that. But now the road had gone. Instead there was a grassy track lined with trees, and they weren't ordinary English trees. There were tall palms and giant redwoods, and thick tangles of green stuff from which most of

the noise was coming – the sounds of jungle insects and birds and animals. The river was still there, but now it was full of water, which rushed madly past the centre, carrying broken branches and even big logs.

The sun was shining down through the leaves, but as Jody watched, the sky – or the little of it she could see – grew dark and there was a flash of lightning and a big clap of thunder, followed by a huge downpour of rain. And while the storm raged, a canoe suddenly came into sight up the river. It was being paddled by Mr Majeika.

Seeing Jody looking out of the window, he waved, paddled himself to the river bank, climbed out – carrying a large basket – and tied up the canoe. The rain hadn't stopped, and when he came into the centre he was dripping wet.

"I thought I'd just go along the river and check that everything was all right," he explained. "Do you like what I've done?"

"Mr Majeika, it's marvellous," said Jody. "It's your best spell ever." And she went off to dress and to wake up the others, who were amazed when they saw the jungle and the swollen river. Even Hamish Bigmore could only say, "Coo!"

"And now," said Mr Majeika, "it's time for your trip. There are enough canoes for everyone, so have a quick breakfast, then put on your life jackets and off you go."

"Aren't you coming with us, Mr Majeika?" asked Thomas.

Mr Majeika shook his head. "I've just got one or two things to do first, but I won't be far behind you. Here's your breakfast – I've just picked it."

From the basket, he took bunches of

bananas and coconuts, and handed them
round.

They all ate the delicious bananas and
split the coconuts and drank the milk that
was inside. Then they put on their life
jackets and climbed into the canoes,

which were made of hollowed-out tree trunks.

"This is going to be a real adventure!" said Pete.

Paddling the canoes wasn't as easy as it looked. There were four people in each one and if anyone paddled harder than the rest, the canoe raced towards the side of the river rather than keeping on straight down.

Jody, Thomas and Pete were cross to find that they had to share a canoe with Hamish Bigmore. Of course he immediately made a nuisance of himself. He either paddled too fast, so that they hit the bank, or stopped paddling altogether, complaining that he was too tired and his arms were hurting. It was impossible to keep the canoe straight while he was on board.

Then there were the rapids. Mr Majeika had warned them about these. "Rapids are when the river suddenly rushes over the rocks," he explained. "You've got to be very careful when you canoe through them, otherwise the canoe will turn upside down and you'll all be thrown into the water."

When Jody, Thomas and Pete saw the

first rapids coming, they told Hamish to be very careful and hold on tight. As they reached the rapids, the canoe began to race forwards. Then it dived down through the rushing water, just missing some sharp, dangerous-looking rocks, before they passed into a calmer stretch of the river.

"Phew," said Pete. "That was frightening."

"It was great," shouted Hamish. "Didn't I handle the canoe brilliantly?"

"Don't be silly, Hamish," said Jody. "You didn't do anything and neither did we. We just left the canoe to find its own way through the rapids."

"Rubbish!" shouted Hamish. "Look, there're some more rapids coming up. You watch how I handle the canoe this time. Wheeeee!" And as they reached the rapids, he stood up, waving his paddle in the air and shouting, "I'm the king of the river!"

The canoe swerved and hit some rocks, and Hamish fell sideways, clutching on to the canoe's edge.

"Look out!" yelled the others, but it was too late. The canoe turned upside down, throwing them all into the water.

"I can't swim," shrieked Hamish, thrashing about like a mad whale.

"Don't worry," called Jody, "your life jacket will keep you afloat." But she was worried. The water seethed and bubbled like a boiling saucepan, and they were all being carried down the river at a frightening speed. Then Thomas called out: "Help – a crocodile!"

Sure enough, something long and green and scaly, with eyes like light bulbs, was approaching them in the water. As it opened its enormous jaw, Jody decided

that she would never see her home and
family again.

Then a voice said: "I think you need a
little help, my friends." The crocodile was
speaking to them.

"No, no, we're fine," called Jody, but at that moment she found herself sucked under the water by a hidden current. When she rose to the surface, coughing and spluttering, she felt herself being lifted into the air. The crocodile had plucked her out of the water with its teeth, though it was only gripping her clothes. Twisting itself in the water, it managed to put her gently on to its back.

"Now to rescue the others," it said, and in a moment Thomas, Pete and Hamish were sitting on its back behind Jody. "Are you sitting comfortably?" it asked them.

"Oh yes, thank you very much," said Thomas.

"Are you sure you don't want to eat us?" asked Pete.

"Shut up, stupid," whispered Hamish. "Don't give it ideas."

But the crocodile said: "Certainly not.

I'm a vegetarian crocodile. I only eat bananas and other fruit."

"That's a relief," said Jody. "Now, please would you be very kind and take us back to the outdoor activity centre?"

"If you really want me to," said the crocodile. "But when Mr Majeika asked me to keep an eye on you, he said I could take you to the Crooked Caves just along the river. Wouldn't you rather go there?"

"That sounds exciting," said Thomas. "Yes, please, do take us to them."

In a few minutes they reached a bend in the river, where the crocodile swam to the shore.

"You can climb off here," it told them. "The Crooked Caves are through those trees. You can't miss them. Goodbye, it was nice to have met you."

They thanked the crocodile, clambered

up on to the river bank and set off through the trees. In a few moments they heard a strange sound, half chanting, half singing.

"It sounds like a football crowd," said Jody. "They seem to be singing 'We are the champions!' "

"Yes, they do," said Thomas, "and what's more, the voices all sound like Hamish Bigmore."

Sure enough, when they came through the trees into a clearing, they found themselves facing a crowd of small people who all looked exactly like Hamish – except that they had painted themselves bright green from top to toe.

"We are the champions!" they were shouting at the tops of their voices. "We are the champions!" They were dancing around a totem pole with a big, ugly face on it.

"I didn't know you had relatives in these parts, Hamish," said Jody, laughing.

But she stopped laughing a moment later. As soon as the bright-green Hamishes saw them, they rushed at them, shrieking wildly. In an instant, they had tied the four of them with ropes, though everyone, especially Hamish, struggled furiously.

"Get off!" he shouted. "Don't you see, I'm just like you? Tie up the others, they're just stupid, but leave *me* alone."

It was no good. The ropes were bound tightly around him, and around Jody, Thomas and Pete, and they found themselves being carried by the green Hamishes towards the mouth of a cave in the hillside a short distance away.

"I think they're taking us into the Crooked Caves," said Jody. "I'm not sure I want to go there after all."

It was very dark inside the cave mouth, but the green Hamishes carried them further and further in, so that soon they were being taken down a crooked, steep, narrow tunnel that ran through the rock.

"We take you to Head Woman," said one of the green men. "Head Woman eat you for her lunch."

"No she won't!" shrieked Hamish. "Take us out of here at once! Fetch stupid old Mr Majeika – it's all his fault."

The narrow passage opened out suddenly into a big underground cave that was lit by a strange green light. In the middle of it stood a giant cooking pot. Beneath it, logs of wood had been laid to make a fire, though it hadn't yet been lit.

"Oh dear," said Thomas. "I've seen pictures of this happening. They put you in the pot, fill it up with water, and then they light the fire and cook you."

When he heard this, Hamish began to shriek even louder.

Suddenly a voice said: "What's the matter with my Star Pupil?"

Jody groaned. "I know that voice," she said. "It's Wilhelmina Worlock."

Wilhelmina Worlock was a wicked witch, and she was always making a nuisance of herself to Class Three and Mr Majeika.

"Tee-hee," she said, coming into the cave and taking her seat on a high throne. The green Hamishes all bowed down before her and chanted, "Head Woman! Head Woman! Head Woman!"

"Are you really going to eat us for lunch, Miss Worlock?" asked Jody.

Wilhelmina scratched her hairy chin. "Perhaps not, dearie," she said.

"Oh, that's a relief," said Thomas.

"I think I'll wait and eat you for tea instead," said Wilhelmina.

"W-w-what about m-m-me?" stammered Hamish. "You wouldn't eat your Star Pupil, would you?"

Wilhelmina always called Hamish her Star Pupil because, unlike the rest of Class Three, he liked her and helped her in her plots against Mr Majeika.

"I'll keep *you* for breakfast," Wilhelmina said to Hamish. "And then I'll eat you on fried bread with ketchup. Tee-hee!"

Hamish went pale. "W-w-why have you turned against me?" he asked, his teeth chattering. "W-w-what have I done to offend you?"

"You've done nothing at all," sneered Miss Worlock. "Star Pupil, indeed! You've never been the slightest use to me against that weasly wizard, Majeika. You're utterly useless. But you might make quite a nice breakfast."

"And so might you, Wilhelmina Worlock," said a voice. It was the crocodile, which had crept silently into her cave without anyone noticing, and had slunk up behind the witch.

Wilhelmina turned and screamed in surprise – and then suddenly she vanished.

The little green Hamishes gasped in
astonishment. The crocodile turned on
them with its jaws open, and in terror
they all ran out of the cave, leaving Jody,
Thomas, Pete and Hamish – still tied up
with ropes – alone with the crocodile.

"The next thing is to untie you all," said

the crocodile, and it used its long sharp teeth to cut through the ropes.

"Thank you very much," said Pete, as they all stood up. "But what's happened to the witch?"

"Wilhelmina?" said the crocodile. "Oh, I just put one of my spells on her."

"Spells?" said Jody. "I didn't know crocodiles could do spells."

"Crocodiles?" said the crocodile. "Oh, sorry, I forgot I was still a crocodile." And it changed into Mr Majeika.

"So it was you all the time?" asked Thomas.

"Yes," said Mr Majeika. "I was worried about how Hamish might behave in the canoe. And I had a feeling that Wilhelmina Worlock might turn up. So I came along to keep an eye on you."

"And what has your spell done to Wilhelmina, Mr Majeika?" asked Jody.

"Come outside and see," said Mr Majeika.

When they got out into the open air, the green Hamishes were dancing happily round their totem pole. The face on it was different now – it was the face of Wilhelmina Worlock.

"You've turned her into a totem pole!" said Thomas. "That's great – we'll never be bothered by her again."

"I'm afraid we will," said Mr Majeika. "The spell won't last long. We'd better clear out before it wears off. Excuse me if I turn myself back into a crocodile for half an hour – it's the easiest way to take you back."

"It would be even more fun if you turned *us* into crocodiles too, Mr Majeika," suggested Jody. "Then we could swim alongside you."

"But I can't swim!" protested Hamish.

"That's all right, Hamish," said Pete. "Mr Majeika can turn you into a rubber duck, and we'll tie a string round your neck and pull you along with us."

"No!" shrieked Hamish.

But that's exactly what Mr Majeika did.

2. St Barty's For Sale

One morning, Jody, Thomas and Pete arrived at school to see a very smart and expensive-looking car parked outside it. It had a gold-plated radiator and silver-plated bumpers. A chauffeur in a peaked cap was sitting in the driving seat. The number plate was BIG 1.

"Wow! That must have cost a lot," said Pete, looking at the car. "Thousands and thousands and thousands. I wonder who it belongs to."

"BIG 1," said Thomas. "I wonder if it

has anything to do with Hamish Bigmore. Look, there he is."

Hamish was standing proudly by it. "It's the most posh and expensive car in the world," he said. "And it belongs to my cousin, Beresford Bigmore."

"He must be very, very rich to afford a car like that," said Jody.

"Of course he is, stupid," said Hamish. "He's a multi-millionaire. In fact, he's one of the richest people in the country."

"If he's a relative of yours, I bet he's a crook," said Thomas.

"He's not!" shouted Hamish, kicking Thomas on the ankle. Thomas kicked him back, and a fight started.

"Stop it, you two," said Jody. "I want Hamish to tell us how his cousin, Beresford, makes his money."

"He's a property developer," said Hamish.

"What's a property developer?" asked
Pete.

"Don't you know that, stupid?" said
Hamish. "A property developer buys old

buildings as cheap as he can. Then he knocks them down and puts up new houses there. Then he sells the houses and makes pots and pots and pots of money."

"I told you he was a crook," said Thomas. "That's a nasty thing to do. Old buildings should be looked after, not knocked down."

"Rubbish!" shouted Hamish. "Anything old should be knocked down. And so should you." He kicked Thomas again, so the fight started once more.

It was broken up by Mr Majeika, who had just arrived at school. "Hamish, behave yourself," he said, "and, Thomas, leave him alone."

Hamish ran off, sticking out his tongue at Thomas and Mr Majeika.

"I wonder what his cousin, Beresford, is doing here," said Jody, as they walked towards their classroom. "I don't see why a millionaire who makes his money from knocking down old buildings should want to come to our school."

"Something nasty is bound to be going on if there's a Bigmore around," said Thomas. "You can bet on that."

"Look," said Pete, as they passed the window of Mr Potter's (the head teacher) office. "That must be Hamish's cousin in there, talking to Mr Potter. He's wearing a smart suit and smoking an enormous cigar, but he looks exactly like Hamish."

"I wish we knew what he was saying," said Thomas.

"So do I," said Jody.

"I'm sure you could hear them by magic, Mr Majeika, if you tried," said Jody.

"Yes, that's possible," said Mr Majeika. "I know just the spell for it. But I really shouldn't use it. I'm not supposed to do magic at all. I know I don't always keep that rule, but I do try to."

"Oh, please, Mr Majeika," said Jody. "I've got a feeling that Beresford Bigmore is up to something nasty. And maybe you could stop him."

"Very well, just this once," said Mr Majeika. He waved his hands at the window. Sure enough, suddenly they could hear the voices of Beresford Bigmore and Mr Potter.

"I'm offering you a very nice deal, Mr Potter," Beresford Bigmore was saying, as he puffed cigar smoke in Mr Potter's face. "I'm offering you a lot of money for the school buildings. An enormous amount. I'm sure you could use it. And I've got some nice new buildings all ready for you to move into, just up the road."

"But, Mr Bigmore," said Mr Potter, scratching his head, "we really don't want to move to new school buildings. We're very happy in these ones."

"But look how small these buildings are," said Beresford Bigmore. "Look how old they are. The rain comes in and the windows are cracked. And you don't have a playing field, only a tiny little playground."

"The children are very happy here," said Mr Potter. "They like it very much."

"But I'm offering you ten thousand pounds, Mr Potter," said Beresford Bigmore, puffing at his cigar. "Ten thousand pounds, and some very nice new buildings with a big playing field. Just think what the school could do with ten thousand pounds."

"That's true," said Mr Potter. "We could buy a new minibus for taking the children on expeditions."

"Sign here," said Beresford Bigmore, taking a piece of paper from his pocket. "If you do, I'll give you the money right away."

Mr Potter looked very unhappy, but he signed the piece of paper. Beresford Bigmore took out his cheque book.

"Here's a cheque for ten thousand," he said, smiling broadly. "I'm sure you'll all be happy in your new school buildings."

Outside in the playground, Jody said: "This is terrible, Mr Majeika. We don't want to move to some horrid new buildings. Can't you do something to stop it?"

Mr Majeika shook his head. "I don't think I can," he said, "now that Mr Potter has signed and taken the money. And we don't know for certain that Hamish's cousin is up to something nasty."

"Of course he is," said Thomas. "He's behaving just like Hamish, so he must be."

Later that morning, during break, Mr Majeika came up to Jody, Thomas and Pete and said: "I'm sorry to say that Beresford Bigmore is a crook. Or at least

he's cheating Mr Potter and the school. Come and see."

He took them to a corner of the classroom where he had put a large empty glass jar on the table, upside down.

"What's that for, Mr Majeika?" asked Pete.

"It's a crystal ball," said Mr Majeika. "Or at least, it works as one. Anything made of glass does, if you know the right spell." He waved his hands over the jar and murmured some words. Suddenly, the jar grew cloudy and they could see a picture forming in it.

"It's showing us Beresford Bigmore in a smart office," said Jody.

"That's right," said Mr Majeika. "It's his own office and he's talking to his partner, Simon Sleeze. Listen."

In the jar, they could see the two men talking, and by putting their heads near to it, they could hear the voices.

"Ten thousand pounds!" Beresford Bigmore was saying. "That old fool, Potter, let me have his school for only ten thousand pounds. Have you ever heard anything so silly. It's worth about two million."

"Ridiculous," laughed Simon Sleeze. "And what about those new school buildings you've promised him? Not much good, are they?"

"Not much good?" cackled Beresford Bigmore. "They're terrible, Simon, absolutely terrible."

"And now that we're the owners of the old St Barty's school buildings," said Simon Sleeze, "we can knock them down and build houses there, and sell them for millions."

"Millions and millions and millions," giggled Beresford Bigmore. "Oh, if only old Potter knew what a fool he'd been."

"This calls for a bottle of champagne!" laughed Simon Sleeze. "In fact, two or three bottles." And he opened a cupboard and took out the champagne and two glasses.

"You lying crooks," shouted Thomas, though of course Beresford Bigmore and Simon Sleeze couldn't hear him.

"I think we've seen and heard enough," said Mr Majeika. He waved his hands and the picture in the glass jar faded.

"This is awful," said Thomas. "What on earth are we going to do?"

"We're going to lose these buildings and go to the horrid new school," said Pete, "and Hamish's cousin and that horrid man are going to make millions out of it."

"Surely there's something you can do, Mr Majeika?" asked Jody. "Can't you think of a plan?"

Mr Majeika sighed again and shook his head. "I really don't think I can, Jody," he said. "Not yet, anyway."

The new school buildings turned out to be even worse than Thomas, Pete and Jody had expected.

For a start, they were about three miles

away from the old St Barty's, right on the edge of town. Most people in Class Three had always walked to school because they lived very near it. But now they all had to come by car or bus. It was too far to walk.

On the day of the move to the new buildings, it was raining hard. Jody and the others waited at the bus stop, but half an hour went past, with the rain splashing down, and no bus came.

"This is dreadful," said Pete. "My coat is letting the water in and I've got rain in my shoes."

Just then, they saw Beresford Bigmore's car, with its BIG 1 number plate, coming down the road.

"Look, he's giving Hamish a lift to school," said Thomas. "Perhaps he'll give us one too."

They all waved at the car, but when

Hamish saw them he stuck out his
tongue. The car whizzed past, its wheels
splashing dirty water over them.

They shouted angrily at the car, but it
had gone. "Just wait till I get my hands on
Hamish," said Pete.

"Me too," said Thomas. "I'll push him
into the biggest and muddiest puddle I
can find."

"Come on," said Jody. "There's no bus, so we'll have to walk."

It took them nearly an hour to walk to school. When they arrived, soaking wet and very tired, they found that almost everyone else was late as well, so that lessons hadn't started on time. Mr Potter was hurrying around, looking very gloomy and trying to organize things.

"These school buildings aren't new at all," said Jody, looking around her. "They look almost as old as the other ones, and they're far worse."

She was right. The main building was very small and most of the classrooms were outside, in old-looking huts.

"It looks more like a prison camp than a school," said Pete.

The room that had been given to Class Three was the worst of all. Two of the windows were broken and the third was stuck open, so that the rain was blowing in through it. There were no proper desks or tables, just some folding chairs that were mostly broken. And there was no shelf for books and just a single light bulb, which didn't give enough light for reading or writing.

As usual when anything went wrong in Class Three, Melanie started to cry.

"Boo-hoo!" she sobbed. "I want to go back to the old school."

"We all do," said Thomas. "But Mr Potter has sold it to Hamish's horrid cousin, and we'll have to stay here for ever and ever."

"You're talking rubbish," grumbled Hamish. "It's much nicer here than at the old school." But everyone could see that he didn't believe what he was saying.

Mr Majeika did his best to teach Class Three, but they were all cold and wet and uncomfortable, and it was a relief when the bell went for school dinner.

Everyone went into the school hall. At least, they tried to, but it was too small for everyone to fit in. So a queue formed in the passage.

"I hope they manage to feed everyone quickly," said Pete. "I'm starving."

"Me too," said Thomas.

But then Mr Potter came out of the hall into the passage and said: "I'm very sorry, everyone, but there's nothing to eat. I've just heard that our dinner ladies have refused to come and work in these new buildings. They say it's too far out of town. I'll try and get something organized by tomorrow, but I'm afraid you'll all

51

have to go hungry – unless you've brought packed lunches."

Everyone groaned. And no one in Class Three had brought a packed lunch apart from Hamish Bigmore. He sat eating it in a corner of the classroom.

"Yum, yum," he kept saying, but he never offered any of it to the rest of Class Three.

"Can't you do some magic to make things better here, Mr Majeika?" asked Pete.

Mr Majeika shook his head. "I've been trying all morning," he said. "The first thing that I did when I arrived, before you'd all got here, was to have a go at some spells. I tried to find a spell to mend the broken windows and get the other window to shut. And a spell to get us better chairs and tables and better lights, and a bookshelf and all the other things we need. But it wouldn't work. I'm rather worried, to tell you the truth. It seems that I can't do magic in this place."

Class Three groaned. It was bad enough to have lost their nice school buildings and have to come to this dreadful place, but how much worse it was if Mr Majeika couldn't do magic any more.

"Do you mean, Mr Majeika," asked Jody, "that nothing happened when you tried those spells?"

"Not exactly, Jody," said Mr Majeika. "Every time I said one of them and waved my hands, a strange picture came into my mind."

"What sort of picture?" asked Thomas.

"It was very odd," explained Mr Majeika. "I could see an enormous crane, the sort they have on a building site. And from the end of it, on a big chain, was hanging a big metal ball."

"I know what that was, Mr Majeika," said Pete. "It's what they use to knock down old buildings – a crane with a heavy metal ball."

"Goodness," said Jody. "Do you think, Mr Majeika, that it means they've already started to knock down the old St Barty's buildings? Maybe that's why your spells here didn't work – someone or something

was trying to tell you to stop wasting time here and go back to the old St Barty's before it's all been knocked down."

"I think you're right, Jody," said Mr Majeika. "Let's get back there as quickly as we can."

"But there's no bus," said Jody, "and it'll take us ages to walk. By the time we get there, it may be too late."

"This calls for a magic carpet," said Mr Majeika. "Look – that's one thing this classroom has got – a carpet. It's dirty and old, but it should do the job. We'll have to take it outside, because I can't do magic in here. But then you can sit down on it, everyone, hold on tight, and off we'll go."

Beresford Bigmore had just ordered his chauffeur to drive him to the old St Barty's buildings, where the demolition men were due to arrive to start knocking them down. The chauffeur parked the car outside the school gates. Then he got out and held the door open for Beresford.

Simon Sleeze was there already, in his own big shiny car, which had the number plate SS 1. He was opening a bottle of champagne and lighting up a big cigar.

"What a fortune we're going to make, Biggy," he said to Beresford. "I reckon we can build at least twenty houses where these stupid old school buildings are standing, and we can sell them for at least a quarter of a million each. That's five million we'll make."

"Yummy," said Beresford Bigmore. "And look, here come the demolition men."

A crane was rolling towards them along the road. On the side of it was painted "DAN'S DEMOLITION. NOTHING IS TOO BIG FOR US TO SMASH IT UP."

From the end of it there dangled a big
metal ball, such as Mr Majeika had seen
in his mind every time he'd tried to do a
spell.

"Get started!" called Beresford Bigmore
to the demolition men as the crane pulled
up outside the school. "Don't leave a
brick of it standing."

"Righto, mate," called the men, and the crane began to rev up, ready to swing the metal ball.

Just at that moment, there was a whooshing noise and Mr Majeika and Class Three came flying over the rooftops on their carpet.

"I don't believe it," said Simon Sleeze. "It looks like a magic carpet."

"Pay no attention," said Beresford Bigmore. "It's the silly man who teaches my cousin, Hamish. Apparently he thinks he's a wizard and can do magic. He's just a nutter, of course."

The magic carpet landed and Mr Majeika looked at the crane and said: "Yes, that's exactly what I saw."

"Hurry up and do something, Mr Majeika," said Jody. "Look, they're going to swing the metal ball at the school roof. It'll only take two or three bashes to

knock it in completely. And then they'll
start on the walls."

Mr Majeika thought for a moment.
Then he shut his eyes and muttered some
words and waved his hands.

The big metal ball swung – but not at
the school roof. At the last moment it

changed direction – and hit Beresford Bigmore's car.

There was a frightful crash of metal and the car spun over like a toy, on to its roof. It was damaged beyond repair.

"You idiots!" screamed Beresford Bigmore at the men from Dan's Demolition. "That car cost me an absolute fortune. You'll have to buy me a new one."

"Sorry, mate," said the head of the Dan's Demolition team. "Something must have gone wrong with the crane. We'll try again."

The big metal ball swung again – and again it turned away from the school roof. This time it hit Simon Sleeze's car.

"Fools!" he screamed, as the car turned a somersault like the other one had done. "That's another car you owe us!"

But this time the Dan's Demolition man

didn't reply. The crane had begun to shake violently, so that he and the other men were thrown out of it into the road. By the time they had picked themselves up, the crane had set off by itself. It was chasing Beresford Bigmore and Simon Sleeze, its metal ball swinging dangerously at them.

The two property developers ran as fast as they could go. A sheet of paper fell out of Beresford's pocket as he and Simon Sleeze turned the corner and were lost from sight, with the crane close behind them.

"Brilliant, Mr Majeika," said Pete. "One of your best spells. I hope the crane will chase them out of town."

"It will," said Mr Majeika. "And as for this," he added, picking up the sheet of paper, "it's the agreement by Mr Potter to sell the school. So I think we know what to do with *that*." He tore it into little pieces and scattered them to the wind. "So tomorrow, St Barty's will be back in its proper buildings and Hamish Bigmore won't be having any more rides in his cousin's posh car."

"Hooray!" said Jody. "Three cheers for Mr Majeika! And we even got to have a magic carpet ride as well."

3. Just the Job

"My sister has been doing work experience," said Jody in the playground one morning. Jody's sister was older than her and at a bigger school than St Barty's.

"What's work experience?" asked Thomas.

"It's when you have a week off school," explained Jody, "and you're sent to places where people do jobs, and you learn to do a job yourself."

"A week off school?" said Pete. "I like the sound of that."

"Do a job myself?" said Thomas.
"That's great. I'd like to drive a train.
Let's ask Mr Majeika if we can have work
experience too."

Mr Majeika had never heard of work
experience. "But it sounds a good idea,"
he said.

"Could we go and learn to be wizards?"
asked Pete.

Mr Majeika shook his head. "That
wouldn't be allowed," he said. "But
maybe you could do some other jobs."

"I'd like to be a racing driver," said
Hamish Bigmore, and he began to make
racing-car noises. "Brrrrrrrrmmmm-
mmmm! Vrrrrrrrrmmmmmmmm!
Eeeeeeeeewowwwwwwweeeeeeee-
owwwwwwww!"

Soon, everyone had to put their hands
over their ears.

"The trouble is," said Jody, "we don't

look big enough or old enough to do the kind of jobs we'd like. People would just laugh at us if we asked them for real grown-up jobs."

"Ah," said Mr Majeika. "I think I can do something about that."

"Can you, Mr Majeika?" asked Thomas excitedly. "When, when?"

"Maybe tomorrow morning," answered Mr Majeika. "I'll see what I can manage by the time you get to school."

When they came into the classroom next morning, Class Three found there were small glasses of a green-coloured drink set out on the tables.

"One for each of you," called Mr Majeika. "Drink it slowly, or you may feel rather strange."

Everyone started sipping their drink, which tasted quite sweet and rather nice. The moment she had swallowed some of it, Jody had a funny feeling in her legs. She looked down. "I'm getting taller!" she said.

"So am I!" called Thomas.

"I'm not touching Mr Majeika's nasty green drink," said Hamish Bigmore. "I don't want odd things to happen to me."

"In that case," said Pete, who was now almost two metres tall, "you're going to be the smallest person in the class. Hello, ickle baby Hamish!"

He walked over to Hamish, finding he could take big strides with his long legs. Hamish looked up at him crossly.

"Go away," he grumbled, "you look stupid."

Thomas, who was just as tall as his brother, strode over to Hamish as well.

"Hello, little boy," he said to Hamish. "If you drink your nice green medicine, you might grow up to be as big as me."

"Shut up," snarled Hamish, and picked

up his green drink to throw it in Thomas's face. Then he changed his mind and swallowed it in one gulp.

"Ooooo!" he cried, for he had shot up as fast as a lift and was now as tall as Thomas and Pete.

Everyone else in Class Three was getting used to being as tall as a grown-up. In fact, the smallest person in the class was now Mr Majeika.

"What giants you all are," he said. "You'd better get out of here before Mr Potter and the other classes see what's happened. Go off and get your jobs."

"What jobs have you arranged for us, Mr Majeika?" asked Jody.

Mr Majeika frowned. "Arranged?" he repeated. "Was I supposed to arrange them? Nobody explained that to me."

"Never mind," said Pete. "There's lots of adverts for jobs on cards in the window of the post office. Let's go and see what we can get for ourselves."

"Come back at the end of school this afternoon, everyone," called Mr Majeika, as they all went off. "Then I can turn you back to your normal size."

Everyone went down to the post office – everyone except Hamish Bigmore.

"I'm not going to get one of those stupid jobs advertised on one of those stupid cards," he said. "I'm going to get a *real* job. You'll see."

"What sort of job are you thinking of getting, Hamish?" asked Thomas. "Prime Minister? President of the United States?"

"I'll be a millionaire by the end of the day," said Hamish. "Just you wait." And off he went.

They all looked at the cards. One of them said: "Assistant wanted by

Goldilocks the Hairdresser. No experience necessary."

"That sounds fine for me," said Jody. "I know Goldilocks, it's that hairdresser by the station. I'll see you all later." And off she went.

Other cards advertised such jobs as gardening, cleaning, babysitting, and working in shops. Everyone found something they liked, and they all went off to apply for the jobs – except Thomas and Pete.

"I don't want to be a gardener, or a cleaner, or a babysitter, or anything like that," said Thomas.

"At this rate, we won't find a job at all," said Pete. "Look, there's one more card in the corner of the window that no one noticed."

Thomas peered at it. "It says, 'Pop singers wanted urgently. Contact

Shambles Recording Studios, Greentree Street.'"

"Pop singers?" said Pete. "That sounds good. Greentree Street is just round the corner. Off we go."

At half-past two that afternoon, Jody left Goldilocks the Hairdresser and was just going back to school when she noticed the Kosy Korner Kafé. She decided there was just time to buy herself something to eat.

She had sat down and was looking at the menu when she heard a tap on the window. It was Thomas and Pete. Jody beckoned them and they came in and sat down at her table.

"Gosh, you look amazing," Thomas said to her.

"Yes, you look just like a model," Pete said.

"I *am* a model," said Jody. "Have a

glance at these pictures." She put a
bundle of photos on the table.

"Cool," said Thomas. Jody's hair had
been specially cut and waved, and her
face had been made up very cleverly. She
looked super in the photos.

"I was learning to cut people's hair,"
she explained, "when a photographer

turned up to take some pictures to put in the window of Goldilocks. And they all decided that I was the best person to photograph. The photographer was so pleased with the way the pictures came out that he's going to give my name to one of the fashion magazines. I may become a famous model!"

"That's great," said Pete. "But will they want to photograph you when you're back to your ordinary size?"

"I thought about that," said Jody. "I'll ask Mr Majeika to make me taller again. How did you both get on?"

"Look at this," said Thomas, putting a CD on the table. The label said "Twinz".

"Twinz? What does that mean?" asked Jody.

"It's us," said Pete. "We're a band now."

"We're called Twinz because we're twins," explained Thomas.

"We went to this place called the Shambles Recording Studio, and it *was* a shambles – really untidy," said Pete.

"It's run by a record producer who was once a pop singer himself," said Thomas. "He's called Shambling Sid Sutton and he makes lots of wonderful records, but before he's finished them the wires usually get all tangled up, or he loses the tape, and he has to start all over again. That's why he was advertising for more singers."

"And did you really make a record?" asked Jody.

"You bet," said Pete. "We recorded a song called 'Magical Mr Majeika'."

"The words begin like this," said Thomas, " 'Mr Majeika, A magical teacher, Mr Majeika, He's such a wizard, yeah!' "

Jody frowned. "It sounds good," she said, "but I'm not sure Mr Majeika will

want to be on a pop record. He likes to keep it secret about being a wizard."

"Don't worry about that," said Pete. "I don't think the record will get into the top ten. Thomas and I can't really play the guitar properly, and I'm sure Shambling

Sid will lose the tape or something before he can release the record. Still, we've got our own disc of it."

"Shouldn't we be getting back to school?" said Thomas. "Mr Majeika wants us to be there in good time so that he can shrink us to our normal size before school ends."

"I was going to order a Coke and a chocolate biscuit," said Jody. "But nobody's taken my order. They're very slow in this café."

Pete looked around him. "I'm not surprised," he said. "Look who the waiter is."

It was Hamish Bigmore, and he was looking very cross at being seen by Thomas, Pete and Jody.

"Hello, Hamish," said Jody. "Didn't you manage to get a job as a millionaire?"

"Shut up," muttered Hamish.

"You're not going to make even one pound if you don't serve customers," said Pete. "Come on, let's go."

They arrived back at St Barty's a few minutes before the end of school.

"Did you all find good jobs?" asked Mr Majeika.

Everyone said yes. They had worked as window cleaners, computer programmers, bus conductors, restaurant cooks, and all sorts of other things. Only Hamish Bigmore refused to say what he had been doing.

"He's been in the Kosy Korner Kafé," laughed Thomas, "making a million pounds an hour in tips."

"Shut up," mumbled Hamish.

"Now everyone," said Mr Majeika, "time to get back to your normal sizes. I've got a packet of Shrinking Powder

ready for everyone. Swallow it with a
glass of water and it should do the trick."

They opened the packets, put the
powder on their tongues and washed it
down with water. In a few seconds all of
them were back to their normal sizes.

"I miss being tall," said Jody.

"I don't," said Thomas. "I kept falling
over my own legs, they were so long."

"Isn't Mr Majeika clever?" said Pete. "These days, his spells never seem to go wrong."

When Jody woke up the next morning, she felt bright and cheerful, but something seemed to be different about her bedroom. Her bed was huge, as big as a football pitch, and the ceiling was as tall as the roof of a church. When she tried to climb out of bed, she saw that there was a drop of about six metres to the floor.

"Help!" she called out, but no one came.

Then the door of her bedroom opened and her mother looked in. This was terrifying because, though she wasn't a very big woman, she'd become an enormous giant. "Jody! Wake up!" she shouted in a voice like thunder.

"I'm here, Mum," Jody called. "I can't get out of bed – everything is far too big."

"Oh, she isn't here," said her mum, who hadn't heard the tiny squeak, which was all that Jody could make. "She must have gone to school early. And she didn't even have breakfast."

Jody tried shouting again, but her mum went downstairs and didn't come back.

Suddenly Jody realized what must have happened. Mr Majeika's Shrinking Powder had gone on working in the night. She had become very, very tiny – scarcely bigger than a mouse.

Had the same thing happened to all the others in Class Three? If so, how on earth were they going to manage to get to school?

There was a pile of old teddy bears behind the bed – they looked like monsters now – and Jody managed to slide down them on to the floor. But getting dressed was out of the question.

Her clothes, which she had thrown on to the floor the night before, were as big as carpets, and her school bag was large enough for a whole family to live in.

The journey downstairs was a nightmare. She had to jump down each single step of the staircase, and by the time she reached the bottom she was very tired. She could hear her mother doing things in the kitchen, but she decided not

to call out. Even if her mother heard her, she would be so frightened and upset by what had happened that she wouldn't be much use.

Jody decided she must somehow get to school by herself, then Mr Majeika wouldn't get in trouble for putting the shrinking spell on everyone by mistake.

By a stroke of luck, someone had left the front door open a crack – which for Jody, in her tiny state, was as wide as a whole doorway. She was still in her pyjamas, which had shrunk with her, and her feet were bare. Fortunately, it was a warm, sunny day, so she would not get too cold on the way to school.

It usually took her five minutes to walk to school. Today, because she was so tiny, it was almost an hour. She picked her way along the huge pavement. Its surface usually seemed quite smooth, but now it appeared to be made up of big sharp rocks and it was hard to find somewhere that she could safely put her feet. And she had to make her way round giant bits of rubbish.

Now and then, something huge and brown would fall out of the sky. At first she didn't know what it was. Then she saw that the brown things were falling leaves.

A black and white cat the size of a tiger hissed at her from a driveway. Further down the road, she was terrified when she came face to face with a monster with enormous teeth, clutching a huge rock. Then the monster ran up a giant tree and Jody realized it was a squirrel holding a nut.

Then she had to cross the road, knowing that no driver could see her. Two cars, each as big as the *Titanic*, roared past before she dared to run across, and she made it to the other side only a few seconds before another of the enormous machines rumbled by.

When she finally got to school, Mr Majeika – tall as a giant – was standing in a corner of the playground, looking very worried, and turning the pages of his spell book. All the rest of Class Three were standing around his huge feet, hoping that soon he would get them back to their ordinary size. The only person whom Jody couldn't see was Hamish Bigmore.

Suddenly Mr Majeika snapped his fingers. "I've found it!" he said. "I've found a spell which will get things right again. Let's try it at once." He waved his arms and muttered some words.

Nothing happened. "Oh dear," said Mr Majeika. "I'll have to try again."

At that moment, along came Hamish Bigmore. He wasn't tiny like the others. He was still as big as he had been the day before after drinking the green drink.

"Hello, tinies," he said to them all. "That'll teach you all to laugh at me. Well, *I'm* not tiny. I kept some of the green drink and when I got home last night I drank it, so that I've got big and tall again. My parents were very surprised! Now I'll pick you all up and put you in my pockets, and I'll take you to the school dustbin and throw you all in, and the dustmen will come and you'll be tipped into the town rubbish tip. Yah boo sucks!"

He bent down to pick up Thomas, Pete and Jody. But at that moment, Mr Majeika's spell to make them all bigger suddenly worked.

They began to grow. Not just back to their ordinary sizes or as big as they had

been the day before, but far, far bigger. They were turning into real giants.

"Help!" said Thomas, as his neck grew longer and longer. "It's like going up in a lift – except that my feet are still down there at the bottom."

"Hello, clouds," said Pete, poking them to see if they were really made of cotton wool. "And doesn't the school look titchy, from so high up?"

"I suppose this is better than being very, very small," said Jody, "but I'm not sure."

"Help, Mr Majeika!" Thomas called. "Please stop us growing any more or we'll get to the moon."

Down on the ground, Mr Majeika was scratching his head again, while Hamish Bigmore, who had arrived too late for the giant spell to be put on him, was staring up at the rest of Class Three. They were now several times bigger than him.

"It's going to be *us* that pick *you* up, Hamish, and put *you* in the dustbin," shouted Thomas.

"Hush!" called Mr Majeika. "I must get you all back to your proper sizes, before anyone sees." He turned the pages of his spell book. "Ah, here's an emergency spell for shrinking," he said.

He waved his arms and muttered the spell and all of Class Three began to shrink again.

So did Hamish Bigmore.

All the others shrank back to their ordinary sizes. Hamish shrank as much as they had. This meant, of course, that they looked normal, but Hamish was very, very tiny.

"What have you done, you silly old wizard?" he shouted furiously at Mr Majeika. "Turn me back to my right size *at once*."

"Oh, I think that can wait a bit, Hamish," said Mr Majeika. "And perhaps you might like to spend the rest of school today in the rubbish bin yourself, just to see what it's like? No? Then you can just sit quietly in a corner, while everyone else writes down what their jobs were like. Oh, and by the way, somebody has phoned the school, asking for Jody to do some modelling in London. And Thomas and Peter, I've had a note from a Mr Shambles, saying that your record is selling very fast and you might be in the top ten next week. It sounds as if your work experience has been a great success!"